Ghost Class

Find out more spooky secrets about

Ghostville
Elementary

Ghostville Elementary

Ghost Class

by Marcia Thornton Jones
and
Debbie Dadey

illustrated by Jeremy Tugeau

A
LITTLE APPLE
PAPERBACK

SCHOLASTIC INC.
New York   Toronto   London   Auckland   Sydney
Mexico City   New Delhi   Hong Kong   Buenos Aires

ISBN 0-439-42437-2

24 23 22 21 20 19   11 12 13 14 15 /0

Printed in the U.S.A.   40
First printing, October 2002

For Allison and Jared Thornton
— MTJ

To Terril Hill,
best wishes with your writing
— DD

Contents

Ghost Class

THE LEGEND

*Sleepy Hollow Elementary School
Online Newspaper*

This Just In: Overcrowding Calls for Drastic Action!

Breaking News: Sleepy Hollow Elementary School is packed with desks, chairs, and kids — lots of kids. Extreme measures are called for. Rumor has it that a group of unlucky third graders will have to move their classroom to the basement. Poor kids! Everyone knows the basement is filled with more ghosts than a graveyard on Halloween. The school's nickname *is* Ghostville, after all! Stay tuned as the haunting news develops!

Your friendly fifth-grade reporter,
Justin Thyme

1
Zombies

"What is taking her so long?" Cassidy whispered to her best friends, Jeff and Nina. The three kids leaned against a windowsill and watched as their principal, Ms. Finkle, turned a rusty key in the basement door of Sleepy Hollow Elementary School.

"I can't believe she's making us go down there," Nina whimpered. "It's awful!"

Ms. Finkle smiled a mysterious smile and pointed a daggerlike fingernail into the darkness. "There you go," she said as the door creaked open.

Musty air crept around the third graders' ankles. "It smells like a wet dog," Cassidy said, wrinkling up her nose.

1

"You'd smell like that, too, if you'd been shut up for over a hundred years," Jeff said. Then, with a laugh, he added, "Come to think of it, you and Nina do smell like you've been shut up for a hundred years."

Nina tossed back her long black hair and stuck out her tongue at Jeff, but Cassidy was used to Jeff's smart-aleck remarks. They'd lived next door to each other since they were three. "Ignore Jeff," Cassidy told Nina. "We might as well make the best of this. It's not like we have a choice."

"Your new classroom is just down those stairs," Ms. Finkle told the class.

Mr. Morton, their third-grade teacher, smiled nervously at his students. "Come on class," he said. "Let's begin our great adventure together!"

Nina shuddered as Mr. Morton led the class through the doorway and down the dimly lit steps. She knew the school was overcrowded. There were too many kids and not enough classrooms. The principal's solution was to set up a classroom in the basement. Nina understood. But why did her class have to be the one unlucky enough to get moved? Nina wasn't afraid of anything when it came to sports, but she was a regular chicken about things like ghosts, spiders, scary movies, and dark basements.

She looked around. Nobody seemed very happy, not even Mr. Morton.

The basement steps creaked and groaned beneath the weight of the kids and their new teacher. A single lightbulb barely lit up the rugged red brick walls and wooden steps. Mr. Morton waved a dictionary in front of him, batting at cobwebs as he went down the steps. "Don't worry," he told the students. "The janitor will get this cleaned up for us in no time."

"Someone should warn Mr. Morton that the basement of Sleepy Hollow Elementary is haunted," Nina whispered to

Cassidy. Nina had never really believed the crazy ghost stories that floated around the school, but she figured if anyplace was haunted, this would be it. Kids called the school *Ghostville* Elementary for a reason.

As soon as the words were out of Nina's mouth, the lightbulb went dead. The kids were plunged into total darkness. For a second there was silence, and then every kid on the steps screamed.

"Stay where you are," Mr. Morton yelled. "And please keep quiet."

Nina grabbed Cassidy's arm and didn't breathe. Suddenly, she felt two cold hands clamp down on her shoulders. When Mr. Morton got the light back on she saw Jeff smiling at her. "Did a ghost get you?" he asked.

"That wasn't very funny," Nina told him. Even though she and Jeff had been friends for a while, he still liked to tease her.

"You guys don't really believe those old ghost stories do you?" Jeff asked. He hopped from foot to foot, anxious to get going.

Cassidy shrugged. She had never actually met a ghost, but that didn't mean they didn't exist.

"This reminds me of a horror movie I saw on TV," Jeff told Cassidy and Nina once the line started moving again. "At the bottom of the steps a zombie jumps out and grabs this girl."

Nina groaned. Cassidy frowned. The basement was creepy enough. They didn't need Jeff, the scary-movie fan, to make it worse. "Be quiet, Jeff," Cassidy said. "And quit tickling my neck."

"I'm not touching you," Jeff said.

Cassidy spun around on the bottom step. Jeff was behind her, but he had one hand on the damp stair rail and his other arm wrapped around his backpack.

The next time someone touched her neck, Cassidy ignored it. She knew it had to be Jeff.

In the hallway at the bottom of the steps, Cassidy felt a cold draft. It felt like it passed right through her body.

That's when Nina screamed.

2
Spiders

Nina's scream cut through the darkness of the hallway.

"What is it?" Mr. Morton asked, rushing toward Nina. "What's wrong?"

"S . . . s . . . something brushed up against my leg," Nina blurted out. "It was big and it was hairy — very hairy."

"Maybe it was a giant spider with eight hairy legs," Jeff said with a straight face.

Nina screamed again. If there was one thing she hated, it was spiders. Everyone knew it.

Mr. Morton patted Nina on the shoulder. "I'm sure it was just a cobweb," he said.

"Don't spiders make cobwebs?" Jeff asked in his most innocent voice.

Cassidy put her arm around Nina's

9

shoulders. Darkness had never bothered Cassidy. She figured if she kept close to her friend, Nina wouldn't be so scared.

"There's nothing to be afraid of in this basement," Mr. Morton said again with a shaky smile before glaring at Jeff. "Stop teasing, Jeff," Mr. Morton warned. Lots of teachers said that to Jeff. It had never worked before and Cassidy had the feeling it wasn't going to work for Mr. Morton, either.

Just then, Cassidy felt something big and cold press up against the back of her leg. "Someone's got me!" She screamed and whirled around. Nothing was there.

Mr. Morton put his hands on his hips. He was about to say something when another kid hollered. "Something slimy licked my finger."

The twins, Carla and Darla, yelled at the same time, "Somebody pushed us."

"Stop kidding around," Mr. Morton said firmly. "This joke has gone on long enough. Now, let's go look at our new room."

Cassidy hadn't been joking. Someone or something really *had* grabbed her leg.

Cassidy swallowed hard and went into the classroom. Dust floated in the weak light from the dirty half-windows. The

room had a cracked chalkboard covered by years of dust. Rows of mismatched furniture filled the room. Cobwebs fluttered from the water-stained ceiling.

"Oh, great," Nina moaned, "more cobwebs."

"This place looks like a graveyard for old school stuff," Cassidy said.

Jeff looked at the antique desks and shelves. "I wish this *was* a graveyard — a haunted graveyard. I went on a haunted cemetery ride once in Florida that had Dracula and a werewolf. It even had giant bugs."

"I bet this basement is full of giant bugs," Nina complained.

Cassidy, Nina, and Jeff sat near each other in the three oldest-looking desks in the room. As soon as Cassidy sat down, she felt a chill so cold it made her bones ache.

To Cassidy, the school's techno-whiz, the thought of spending an entire year trapped in a musty room sounded like pure torture. The room was dingy and dirty. The map on one end of the chalkboard was so old it didn't even picture all the states.

Mr. Morton didn't seem to notice. He wrote math problems on the chalkboard like it was his favorite thing to do. Soon, a cloud of fine chalk dust poofed around his head and covered his thick black-framed glasses.

Cassidy shook her curly blond hair in disbelief. "What's he doing?" she asked Nina. "Doesn't he know we're supposed to play games for the first week of school?"

Nina was too busy watching a cobweb. She was sure the big black spider stared back at her.

Cassidy sighed and looked around the room for a computer. She gasped. There wasn't a single keyboard to be seen. "What kind of room is this?" she whispered to Jeff. "We don't even have a computer. I feel like we've stepped back in time!"

"Yeah, about one hundred years back in time," Jeff said. "It looks like an old one-room schoolhouse!" His feet were tapping out a nervous patter beneath his ancient desk. Even when he was sitting he had the fastest feet at Sleepy Hollow Elementary.

Cassidy sighed again and checked out the top of her desk. Someone had scratched his name all over it. It was bad enough that Cassidy had to sit in an old, beaten-up desk; she couldn't live with someone else's name written on it.

She gripped her pencil and started trying to erase the marks on her desk. Then she added a few good scribbles of her own.

"Stop messing with my desk!" someone whispered.

Cassidy looked over her shoulder. Everyone in the class had their eyes on their math papers. Even Mr. Morton studied his math book. Cassidy glared at Jeff. It was just like him to play a trick like that. Behind her a boy named Andrew gave her a mischievous smile. He was even more of a troublemaker than Jeff. He could be teasing her, too.

Cassidy went back to doodling her name. The second her pencil tip touched the old wooden desktop, something cold tickled her neck. Cassidy turned around. Andrew wasn't there. He had gotten up to ask Mr. Morton a question. Jeff was flicking erasers off his desk. Everyone else was scribbling down math problems.

Cassidy tried to write her name again, but her pencil tip broke. "This stinks," Cassidy snapped. She took a tiny pencil sharpener out of her backpack and went to the trash can.

The twins, Carla and Darla, sat nearby. "You'd better sit down . . ." Darla whispered to Cassidy. At least, Cassidy thought it was Darla. It could've been Carla.

". . . before you get in big trouble," Carla finished. Or maybe it was Darla.

When Cassidy tried to sit down, it felt like she was sitting on someone's lap. "Yikes!" Cassidy yelped and jumped up.

Mr. Morton peered at her over his math book. "Please take your seat and get to work, Miss Logan," Mr. Morton said.

"Are you okay?" Nina whispered.

Cassidy nodded. She bent over her seat and stared at it.

"What's wrong?" Andrew sneered. "Are you allergic to your chair?" A few kids giggled. Carla and Darla gave Cassidy identical warning glares, but Cassidy ignored them and continued to examine her seat. Her chair looked old, and it was definitely empty.

"This is the stupidest desk in the world," Cassidy snapped and flopped down in her chair. This time, she ended up on the floor. "I'll get you for that, Andrew," she blurted.

Some kids snickered. Andrew laughed out loud. "I didn't do anything, Klutzy Cassidy," he said.

Mr. Morton stood by Cassidy's desk and crossed his arms over his chest. "Enough is enough, Miss Logan," he said. "For disrupting the entire class and writing on school property, you will have to stay inside during recess — all by yourself."

Cassidy looked around the basement room and gulped. She would find out who had moved her chair, and she would get even — if it was the last thing she did.

3
Dust Storm

"Scrub your desktop," Mr. Morton said. "Then write a paragraph explaining the value of school property. I'll check in on you before recess is over." Mr. Morton pushed on a rusty door at the back of the room. It squeaked open and sunlight flooded into the basement.

"Cool," Jeff said. "We have our own escape door to the playground."

Cassidy squeezed out a wet sponge as the other kids filed past her and out the door. "We warned you," Darla said as she passed by. "You'd better behave . . ."

". . . if you ever plan on going outside again," Carla finished.

Nina put her hand on Cassidy's shoulder and smiled. "Kickball won't be the same without you," Nina said.

"That's right," said Andrew. "It will be more fun."

Jeff was the last one out of the room. He laughed an eerie kind of laugh. "Hee, hee, hee! Beware of the ghosts of Sleepy Hollow!" he teased.

Cassidy felt like throwing the cleaning sponge at him, but figured she'd only get in more trouble. She sighed and scrubbed the top of her old desk, muttering with every stroke. "It's not fair! It's not my fault!" The more she scrubbed, the louder she muttered. "Whoever pulled out my chair should be doing this."

"Hah!"

Cassidy heard a deep belly laugh. She dropped her sponge and held her breath. Someone was laughing right in her ear.

Cassidy looked behind her. No one was there! She looked all around the room. She peered under the teacher's desk. In fact, she searched under every desk. There really wasn't anyone there. A chill slithered down her back.

"This creepy basement must be getting to me," she said out loud. "I'd better finish this fast."

Cassidy rubbed her name off the desk. Presto! It disappeared. Then she worked on the name that had been written years and years ago: Ozzy. "What kind of name is that?" she muttered. It had been there so long it was almost worn off anyway. "Good-bye, Ozzy," Cassidy said. She squirted the cleaner at Ozzy's name and scrubbed. "This is my desk, now."

Wham! The door slammed and the curtains snapped shut. A cold wind whipped through the room causing a hundred years of chalk dust to churn across the room in a white funnel cloud.

Shapes flew around and around in the dust cloud. Whispers filled the air. "Leave our room! Leave our room!" The whispers grew louder and louder. "LEAVE OUR ROOM ALONE!"

The dust cloud twirled around Cassidy. She covered her ears with her hands and

tried to block out the noise, coughing as more dust swirled through the room. Dust covered her from the tip of her blond head to the soles of her blue sneakers. Cassidy wiped at the dust covering her face. Then the lights went dead and she was left in complete darkness.

4
Ghost?

Cassidy stumbled over to the wall and flipped on the light switch. She spun around to see a boy about her age, sitting in her desk. He had dark hair that stuck up on top. He wore denim overalls and a striped shirt with a collar. She stared at his tattered shoes until his laughter made her look into his brown eyes.

"How did you do that?" Cassidy asked the boy, but he wouldn't stop laughing. "That wasn't funny at all," she told him.

She stepped toward the desk. "You'd better quit laughing," she warned. She reached over to grab him, but her hand closed around nothing except air — very cold air.

Cassidy's mouth dropped open as she hugged her own dusty arms. She had

never felt such a chill. For the first time, Cassidy noticed that the boy wasn't normal. He shimmered around the edges. He was so pale that Cassidy could see right through him. He reminded her of a glowing green-frosted bubble. The boy stood up from the desk and in that instant, he disappeared.

"Where did you go?" Cassidy asked. "Come back here."

The room was still except for a whisper. "I'm warning you. Leave my desk alone."

At first, Cassidy was scared. Had she really seen a ghost? Then Cassidy got mad.

Dust covered every surface of the classroom. Mr. Morton would think she did it. "Come back here and clean up this mess!" Cassidy stomped her foot, sending a little dust cloud into the air above her sneakers. She may as well have been talking to the wind, because the boy didn't reappear.

"This is just great," Cassidy snapped. "Some kids get pen pals — I get a ghost bully."

Suddenly, a noise made Cassidy freeze. Maybe the ghost was back! She whirled around. Jeff and Nina stood at the door to the playground.

"Did you guys see that?" Cassidy asked.

"See what?" Jeff and Nina said together.

"The ghost boy," Cassidy told them.

Jeff laughed. "Yeah, right. I think I just saw a ghost boy skateboarding around the playground."

Nina put her hand on Jeff's shoulder. "I think she's serious. Cassidy really saw something."

"I'm serious, too." Jeff said with a grin. "Serious about the trouble Cassidy's going to be in when Mr. Morton sees this mess. Maybe the Ghostville ghost can help you blast this mess away," he teased.

Cassidy glared at Jeff as she stomped

to the back of the room to grab a mop. "I'm not joking," she said. "I just saw a ghost right here in this very classroom."

Jeff tossed a dust mop to Cassidy. "Next you'll think that mop is a dancing skeleton."

"It's not fair," Cassidy mumbled as she swished the mop across the floor. "Not fair. Not fair. Some ghost made the mess and I have to clean it up. Not fair. Not fair. Not fair."

Cassidy stomped on the mat by the back door extra hard. She was so mad she didn't notice that something weird was happening — the little rug underneath her feet was bunching up all on its own. It wiggled, it squirmed, it bubbled, it scrunched. Suddenly, Cassidy teetered. Then she fell down right on the seat of her pants.

From somewhere in the empty basement came the sound of laughter.

5
Olivia

From the hall, the kids heard a jingle. Or maybe it was a jangle. Olivia, the head custodian, appeared at the door. Keys swayed from her pocket, earrings dangled close to her shoulders, a heavy toolbelt rode low on her hips, and bright red sneakers peeked out from beneath red overalls.

"I thought I heard something," Olivia boomed in her regular voice. "I wondered what I might find in here."

All the kids knew Olivia. She had been the custodian at Sleepy Hollow Elementary for as long as even their parents remembered. She was known for finding stray animals. Today, Olivia cradled a turtle in her hands. The turtle peered up at her with bright black eyes while Olivia stared at the room.

Cassidy knew it didn't look good. Dust and paper littered the floor. A few chairs were turned upside down.

"Look at this mess," Olivia said. Her voice was louder than normal, causing the turtle's head to disappear inside its shell. Olivia gently stroked the turtle's back. "You're going to have to clean this up, you know," she told Cassidy, Nina, and Jeff.

"But I didn't do it," Jeff said.

"He's right," Nina said. "We were outside playing kickball." Nina's grass-stained knees proved that she was telling the truth.

Jeff raised his eyebrows and looked at Cassidy. So did Nina and Olivia. Even the turtle looked at Cassidy.

"I didn't make this mess, either," Cassidy snapped. Then she glared at Jeff. "Some friend *you* are," she muttered.

Olivia hushed the kids with a look.

"Kids need to get along," she added. "ALL kids. That should be your goal. That and not making messes."

Jeff, as usual, didn't listen. "My goal is to eat as much candy and watch as many monster movies as possible. The only messes I make are with candy wrappers."

"But I didn't do it," Cassidy sputtered. "You have to believe me!"

Nina tossed her long hair back and stood by her friend. "I believe you." They had been in the same class every year since first grade. If Cassidy said she didn't do it, that was good enough for Nina.

Olivia looked at the topsy-turvy chairs. She ran a finger over a dust-covered desk. She kicked a pile of paper scattered on the floor. "Next you'll be telling me ghosts did this," Olivia said with a wink.

Olivia laughed so hard her tools clinked and her earrings clanked. Or maybe the tools clanked and the earrings clinked. Then Olivia and her turtle were gone.

Cassidy wanted to tell her friends

more about the ghost. Maybe together they could figure out how to get rid of it. But she didn't have a chance because Mr. Morton and the rest of the class filed in through the back door.

Mr. Morton took one look at the room and his ears turned red. "What happened?" he sputtered as he rubbed dust from his glasses.

Before Cassidy could say a word, the old map hanging over the chalkboard snapped up. Written on the chalkboard in blocky letters were three words:

6
Ghost History

That afternoon, Mr. Morton's eyes lit up. "Uh-oh," Cassidy muttered. Teachers always had that look when they were planning a huge assignment.

Cassidy sighed. She already had to write a paper about proper behavior because of the mess the ghost made. She didn't need any more work.

Mr. Morton stopped smiling long enough to hunt around the room. "Where's my chalk?" he asked.

A couple of kids shrugged their shoulders. A boy named T.J. looked under the desks. Carla and Darla looked at Cassidy. "I didn't take it," Cassidy said. "Honest."

Carla waved her hand in the air. "We'll go to the office . . ."

"... the principal keeps extra supplies there," Darla added.

Mr. Morton smiled at the twins. "That

would be very helpful, girls," he said. "Helpful students are exactly what this class needs." He glanced at Cassidy to make sure she got the point. Cassidy's day was going from bad to worse.

"Maybe the ghost took the chalk to play hopscotch," Jeff teased Cassidy. He laughed at his own joke.

No sooner were Carla and Darla out of the door than two lunch boxes fell off the shelf in the back of the room. They landed with a clatter that made the whole class jump.

"I didn't touch them," Cassidy said quickly. Then she looked at Jeff. "The ghost did it," she mouthed.

Jeff laughed. "Maybe ghost boy is sick of cafeteria food," he whispered.

As soon as Carla and Darla came back with a big box of chalk, Mr. Morton got that excited-teacher gleam in his eyes again. "It's time for social studies," he said, rubbing his hands together. "Please take out your books. I can't wait to get started on our new project!"

Cassidy sighed and dug through her desk, looking for her book. She knew it was in there. But no matter how hard she looked, she couldn't find it.

Cassidy scooted over to share with Nina. "It's the ghost," Cassidy whispered. "He took my book. He's trying to get me in trouble."

Nina shivered. Cassidy seemed so serious. Maybe she really had seen a ghost. "What did he look like?" Nina asked.

Mr. Morton interrupted their whispers. "Today, we start a new assignment. We'll be doing group projects about local history!" Mr. Morton said it as though he expected the entire class to break into cheers and applause. When they didn't, he continued, though his smile wasn't quite as big as before. "Each group will be reporting about something in our community. You get to choose your group, and your group will choose the topic."

As soon as the words were out of his mouth, kids dashed back and forth, picking partners. Mr. Morton clapped his hands for order, but it was useless. Everyone wanted to work with their friends. Cassidy pulled Nina and Jeff to a back corner.

"There *is* a ghost in our classroom," Cassidy whispered.

"There's never been any *real* proof that this school is haunted," Jeff said, sitting cross-legged on the floor. "But it would be cool if it was."

"How do we know for sure it isn't?" Nina asked, with her eyes wide. "No one other than Olivia has been down here for over one hundred years. And you have to admit it was weird when that rug tripped Cassidy."

"Yeah, and the school's nickname *is* Ghostville," Cassidy added.

"But its real name is *Sleepy* Hollow Elementary," Jeff said. "Our school is the sleepiest school ever. It's too boring to have ghosts."

"Our school," Mr. Morton said as he passed by the three kids. "What a great topic for your project. You can report on the history of Sleepy Hollow Elementary."

Cassidy and Nina moaned. Jeff's mouth fell open. He looked up at Mr. Morton, but there was no sense arguing. Mr. Morton was already off to another group.

Nina slapped her hand on her knee. "I wanted to write about the Sleepy Hollow Bullets. At least the school's baseball team is a fun topic."

"We'll have the world's most boring report," Jeff complained, "about the world's most boring school. Nothing interesting ever happened here."

"What about the ghosts?" Cassidy asked.

Jeff rolled his eyes. "That's just a

bunch of baloney. Spooky noises late at night, kids getting sucked into the basement and never being heard from again. The stories aren't even cool."

Nina gasped and looked around the room, but Cassidy was determined. "The ghosts are part of the history of our school," Cassidy said. "We'll do exactly what Mr. Morton wants us to. We'll find out about our school's history — the ghost history!"

7
The Last Laugh

"What's wrong with you?" Jeff asked Cassidy on the walk home. "You look like a dinosaur pooped on your homework."

"We have to talk," Cassidy said, "at my house."

"As long as you have peanut butter sandwiches, I'll listen." Jeff told her. "I'm so hungry I could eat California."

"Me too," said Nina, jumping up and down. "And I need to use the bathroom."

"Just don't tell my grandfather about the ghosts in our new classroom," Cassidy said. "I don't want to upset him."

The kids politely said hello to Cassidy's grandfather while Cassidy slapped together sandwiches and grabbed some other snacks. Cassidy's grandfather had lived with her family for the last two years. He had a habit of listening in on her friends' conversations. To make sure he couldn't hear, Cassidy herded Nina and Jeff into the backyard.

"We have a problem," Cassidy told her friends as she sat down on the grass. "I am not sharing a room with a ghost for the rest of the year."

Jeff grinned and held up a peanut butter-covered hand. "Maybe your ghost just wants to have some fun."

"Ghosts should not have fun," Nina said firmly. "Ghosts should stay in dark places and leave us alone. We have to warn Mr. Morton."

Jeff shook his head. "He would never believe it. I'm not sure I believe it, either. If there really is a ghost, why is Cassidy the only one that can see him?"

Cassidy shrugged. "Because for some reason he decided to pick on me. But that's not the point. We have to get rid of

the ghost ourselves before he does some real harm."

"Can ghosts really hurt people?" Nina asked. All the color had drained out of her face.

"Nobody really knows all the things ghosts can do," Jeff said, after licking peanut butter off his fingers. "In this one movie I saw, the ghost gained energy from things that used to belong to him. The ghost didn't want strangers moving into his old house, so he gathered strength from an old hammer. It was like a battery charger for him. He used his hammer to smash all the family's stuff into smithereens. It was cool."

"Our room is *full* of old things," Nina said, her voice shaking just a little. "If that movie is right, the ghost could be gaining strength from anything!"

"And it's up to us," Cassidy said with a determined nod, "to get rid of whatever it is."

"This is starting to get interesting," Jeff said, rubbing his hands together. "We could make a video about our very own classroom ghost."

"I thought you didn't believe there was a ghost," Cassidy said to Jeff. She raised an eyebrow and smiled, waiting for Jeff to answer.

Jeff finally shrugged. "A ghost report is more fun than a history report, even if the ghost isn't real."

"This isn't one of your scary movies," Nina said, pointing her sandwich at Jeff. "This is real-life and we don't have any superhero magic."

"We may not have magic," Cassidy said slowly, "but we do have power. I know just where we can find out how to get rid of our ghost pest — the museum."

Cassidy led the way down the street to the old house that was the town's museum. A rusty sign out front read:

Sleepy Hollow Local History Museum

"Why did you bring us here?" Jeff complained. "This place is filled with nothing but old junk." He tapped his foot on the hard floor while Cassidy sat at a computer. She quickly did a search for "Classrooms Through the Ages."

"Because information can give us the power to get rid of our ghost pest. Check this out," Cassidy said. "These desks look like ours and they're from 1870."

"Isn't there a video or DVD we could check out instead?" Jeff asked as he moved toward the door. "Looking at old furniture on a computer screen is boring."

"Wait," Nina told Jeff. "When our ghost was alive, there were no movies, no videos, no telephones, and no cars. He couldn't go home and watch television."

"No videos," Jeff moaned. "What did he do for fun?"

"He played tricks on people," Cassidy said, her mouth set in a grim line.

"At least your ghost has a sense of humor," Jeff said. "That's more than I can say about you right now."

"I'm not laughing because this isn't funny," Cassidy snapped. "But maybe we can have the last laugh. Just maybe we can out-trick the ghost."

"What do you have in mind?" Nina asked.

8
Cassidy's Plan

Jeff held his nose when he and Cassidy met up with Nina on the way to school early the next morning. "What's that horrible smell?"

"Garlic," Nina said. "It's to scare away the ghost. Just in case Cassidy's plan doesn't work."

"The only thing you're going to scare away with that is your friends," Jeff said with a laugh.

Cassidy held her nose, too. "I'm pretty sure garlic is for vampires — not ghosts," she told Nina.

Nina pulled the garlic off her neck and tossed it into the nearest trash can. "I worried about Cassidy's ghost all night. I thought the necklace might help."

"I've got all we need right here," Cassidy said, patting her backpack. "That ghost doesn't like me and I don't like him right back, but I'm going to win this ghost war."

"It might not be a good idea to get into a battle with a ghost," Jeff warned Cas-

sidy as they made their way across the playground. A lone swing swayed in the cool breeze, its squeaking chain slicing through the morning air. "Ghosts can change their form. They can even turn into monsters."

Nina shivered and hugged her arms. "Jeff is right. I don't want to fight any ghosts."

Cassidy faced her friends. "I don't want to fight a ghost, either. I don't want to have anything to do with ghosts. But it's too late — the ghost started it."

"I brought my dad's old video camera just in case ghost boy shows up," Jeff said, adjusting the strap on his backpack. "It might come in handy for our report."

"All right," Cassidy said. "Let's do it." Nina was so afraid to go down the steep steps leading from the playground to their classroom, Cassidy and Jeff had to grab her by the elbows and carry her down.

"Maybe we should just forget about this," Nina said. "We could ask our parents to send us to boarding schools instead."

Cassidy didn't answer Nina. She stared into the classroom at the ghost boy perched on top of her desk. He stuck his fingers in his mouth to stretch it into a gruesome grin.

"Don't you see him?" Cassidy hissed, just loud enough for Nina and Jeff to hear.

"Who?" Nina asked, squeezing in the doorway beside Jeff.

"The ghost boy!" Cassidy pointed to her desk.

"They can only see me if I let them," the boy said. "And you can just get out of here. All of you!"

At that instant, the ghost boy glowed green from head to toe, showing himself to Nina and Jeff for the first time. Nina screamed and Jeff slumped against the door.

"I think I'm going to be sick," Nina moaned.

"I see him," Jeff gasped. "There really is a ghost!"

"And he's getting out of here!" Cassidy yelled. "This is our room. No ghosts allowed." She pulled a crumpled piece of paper out of her backpack and held it up for the ghost boy to read:

NO GHOSTS ALLOWED!

The ghost boy stomped his foot and flew to the chalkboard. He wrote in shaky letters:

No Peeple Allowed!

This time, Cassidy stomped *her* foot. She pulled a portable blow-dryer out of her backpack. She quickly plugged it in and turned it on full blast. "If you won't leave on your own, then I'll blow you away."

Jeff and Nina held their breaths, and the ghost boy did, too. In fact, he filled his cheeks with air. They grew bigger and bigger. Soon his entire head was the size of a basketball. Then it grew to the shape of a watermelon. The ghost boy's head looked like it would pop at any minute.

Cassidy's knees trembled. Her stomach did triple somersaults. Her heart beat hard inside her chest.

A grin stretched across the ghost boy's growing head. "Boo!" he shouted with a giant *whoosh* that blew Cassidy's hair straight back. Nina and Jeff fell against the wall. Pages of books flapped in the whirlwind. The map fell from the chalkboard. Papers fluttered off Mr. Morton's desk.

Cassidy shrieked and dived to the floor along with all the papers from their teacher's desk just as the classroom door flew open.

9
A Hairy Ghost

"What happened?" Olivia asked from the hall doorway.

Cassidy jumped and Nina let out a little shriek. Jeff looked all around, but the ghost boy was gone. Jeff hadn't even had a chance to take out his video camera.

"I didn't mean to startle you," Olivia said. "I found this poor little kitty-cat shivering behind the Dumpster out back. I named him Mo and thought I'd let him rest down here where it's nice and warm."

With a jingling and jangling of her keys, Olivia stepped inside the room. Huddled in her arms was a cat as black as night. Mo's yellow eyes widened for an instant. Then he hissed and sprang straight from Olivia's arms.

Mo dashed first one way, then another,

as if something was trying to catch him by the tail. The cat tore across the room. Desks, chairs, books, papers, and a globe fell to the ground.

Olivia and the kids tried to catch the cat, but whenever they came close it felt like someone tripped them. Finally, poor frightened Mo darted out the door and down the hall. The kids helped Olivia up.

Before Olivia left, she pointed to the mess. "It's time you started getting along in this room — ALL of you. And that means sharing. You had best sweep up those kitty-cat paw prints, too," she said with a wink of her eye.

The kids looked to where Olivia had pointed. There, scattered in the chalk dust on the floor, were lots of cat prints. There was also a larger set of paw prints — the kind a big dog would make.

The three kids looked at each other. "Uh-oh," Nina said. "Those paw prints look like they belong to a dog. A ghost dog!"

"Maybe," Jeff said slowly as he straightened the papers on Mr. Morton's desk, "the ghost and his dog don't want to share the room with us, just like the ghost in that movie I saw. This *was* the ghost's room for over a hundred years. I bet he wants to keep it the way it was."

Nina looked like she might cry. "It's almost sad, when you think of it that way. Maybe instead of fighting with the ghost, we should try talking to him nicely."

Cassidy smiled a pretend smile. "Of

course! We could summon the ghost and have a pizza party," she said.

Nina grabbed Cassidy's arm. "Think about it. This ghost and his dog have been stuck here with their stuff for a long, long, *long* time. It's the only home they have and they're afraid of losing it."

"That's it!" Cassidy yelled. "I know what we need to do!" She grabbed her heavy wooden desk and started pulling it toward the door.

"What are you doing?" Nina asked.

"If we get rid of all the old stuff in the room, the ghosts will be powerless," Cassidy said.

Jeff laughed. "So we really will out-trick the ghosts." He grabbed the other side of Cassidy's desk and helped her tug it toward the door.

"You'd better hurry before Mr. Morton gets here," Nina said.

"NO! NO! NO!" The words echoed all around the classroom. "That's my desk!"

"Not anymore," Cassidy said, giving the desk a shove.

Splat! A tuna fish sandwich slammed into Cassidy's face. "Hey, that's my lunch!" Cassidy screamed and wiped the tuna off her face.

An invisible hand lifted a juice bottle, a granola bar, and an apple out of Cassidy's lunch box. *Whack! Bam! Fling!* The food pelted Cassidy in the face and arms.

"Food fight!" Jeff laughed as his own lunch was pulled from his backpack.

"Quit it!" Cassidy yelled and held her arms up to protect herself.

Nina raced over to help Jeff get the desk out of the room, but she was pelted by food, too. In fact, food came from every direction. All three kids hid their faces.

"There's more than one ghost!" Jeff screamed.

Suddenly, the food stopped flying and

the kids stared at each other. Cassidy was covered with chocolate milk. Nina's black hair had lettuce all over it. Jeff had salami on his head and yogurt on his shirt. "You look like an exploding sandwich," Cassidy told Jeff. They all giggled until the door swung open. There stood Mr. Morton and he didn't look happy.

10
Trouble

"Your war with the ghosts is getting us nothing," Jeff told Cassidy later that day. "Nothing but trouble. The first week of school and we already have detention. It's a new record."

The class was in the library, gathering information for their projects on local history. Jeff had checked out some videos. Nina had looked through the reference section. Cassidy had searched online. Now they were huddled around the computer with a bunch of old school scrapbooks spread out in front of them.

"You're right. It looks like I'm stuck with that old desk," Cassidy said. "We have to think of another way to get the ghosts out of our classroom."

"What if the ghosts are in the library

right now?" Nina asked, glancing over her shoulder. "They'd be mad if they knew we were still plotting against them."

"Since when do you worry about how a ghost feels?" Cassidy asked.

Nina's face turned red and she quickly opened one of the old school scrapbooks.

"Don't worry," Jeff said as he tapped his feet on the carpet. "All the old stories talk about the ghosts being in the basement. They never mention anything weird happening in the rest of the school."

Cassidy looked at the computers and the metal shelves. "The library looks too modern to be haunted," she said. "But how can that be? Doesn't the plaque on the school say Sleepy Hollow was founded in 1850?"

"This building can't be that old," Jeff said. "It has air-conditioning and electricity."

Nina flipped through the yellowed pages of the scrapbook in her lap until something caught her eye. "Look at this

newspaper article," she said. "It's about the dedication of the new Sleepy Hollow Elementary School. It says the new school was built on the site of the original school, and that it will be 'a lasting memorial to the terrible occurrence in 1870.'"

"Terrible occurrence?" Jeff asked.

"What happened to the old school?" Cassidy asked.

"It doesn't say," Nina told her. "But there's a picture of it." She held up the faded photo of kids inside an old one-room schoolhouse. The caption under the picture listed their names. One of the names was Ozzy.

"That's the name scratched into my desk," Cassidy said. "I bet he's the ghost haunting our classroom."

A dog named Huxley stood at attention in the photograph. "According to the article," Cassidy said. "Huxley was devoted to the kids, following them wherever they went. He was so loyal the teacher even let him stay in the class-room."

"I always wanted a dog," Nina said. "But I never thought it would be a ghost dog."

"At least with a ghost dog you won't have to worry about a pooper-scooper," Jeff said with a laugh.

Cassidy didn't laugh. "We still have to find a way to get rid of our ghosts," she said.

"Maybe we should try to get along with them," Nina said. "Remember what Olivia told us? Kids need to get along. *All* kids."

"I'm sure she didn't mean ghost kids," Jeff said.

Cassidy stared at Nina for a long time. She tapped her fingers on the computer keyboard. "That's it!" Cassidy yelled. "I've got it!"

11
Ghost Solution

"I have the perfect solution to our ghost problem," Cassidy told her friends. She leaned over the library table and told them her plan.

"What if Mr. Morton doesn't buy it?" Jeff asked.

"There's only one way to find out," Cassidy said. "Let's go!"

Cassidy grabbed the hall pass and took off running, but Jeff and Nina quickly overtook her. They were all out of breath when they barged into the classroom.

"We have a plan," Cassidy said between gulps of air.

"Plan?" Mr. Morton asked suspiciously.

Cassidy and her friends huddled around Mr. Morton's desk. They spread the scrapbook out in front of him. Cassidy pointed to one particular picture. Mr. Morton wiped away a small circle of chalk dust from his glasses and a slow smile etched across his face.

"Perfect," he said. Then he erased the spelling words he had written on the chalkboard and filled the space with the kids' plan.

"Do you really think this will work?" Jeff asked.

Cassidy shrugged, but when she didn't see Ozzy or Huxley for the rest of the day she had a feeling that it would.

That weekend, all the kids and their parents helped out with Cassidy's idea. Even Ms. Finkle, the principal, got to work with a paintbrush and dust rag. When it was finished, everyone cheered.

The new-old-classroom looked great, and it looked almost exactly like the picture of the one-room schoolhouse in the scrapbook. Ms. Finkle had found enough antique desks for the whole class, and even Mr. Morton's desk was raised like the one in the photo. Copies of old pictures borrowed from the museum hung on the wall. Cassidy's mom had brought in an old coal stove. They didn't use it for heat, but it made a good place to store glue and art supplies.

"It looks like something from a museum . . . ," Darla said.

". . . a living museum," Carla added.

Andrew thumped Cassidy on the head. "Who would ever believe the classroom klutz could think up something this good?"

"Nobody else has a classroom like this," Jeff admitted.

Cassidy had to agree. Their room was pretty cool, especially since it now had a few modern-day things, like computers, a television, and an electric pencil sharpener.

Olivia nodded her approval. She nodded so hard her earrings jingled. Or maybe they jangled. "Fit enough for kids of today — and kids from yesterdays," she said with a wink. "Living or otherwise."

Ms. Finkle pointed upstairs. "Let's celebrate the completion of the room with treats in the cafeteria." All of the kids cheered.

Cassidy, Nina, and Jeff stayed behind when everyone else headed upstairs. They waited until Ozzy, the ghost boy, slowly materialized at Cassidy's desk.

"How do you like the room?" Nina asked.

Ozzy smiled and glanced around. The kids looked, too. That's when shimmering clouds began to take shape. There weren't just one or two. There was a whole class of ghosts sitting in, on, or around the old-fashioned desks. Huxley, the ghost dog, wandered to the front of the room and sniffed the trash can.

Nina started to scream, but her voice was caught in her throat. Jeff grinned. Cassidy felt like she had just swallowed

a bowling ball. Then Ozzy winked and disappeared with all the other ghosts.

"Do you think they'll be back?" Nina whispered.

Cassidy nodded. She had a feeling their ghost adventures were just beginning.

Ready for more spooky fun?
Then take a sneak peek at the next

Ghostville Elementary

#2 Ghost Game

"It's all right," Jeff said, pulling a light cord. "It's just a janitor's closet."

The two girls followed Jeff inside the room. "Is Olivia in here?" Cassidy asked.

"Olivia?" Nina called again.

The only answer was the slam of the door. Cassidy grabbed the doorknob, but it wouldn't budge. "We're trapped!" she said with a gulp.

Nina looked at the iguana squirming in Jeff's hand. "We're trapped in a closet with an iguana monster," Nina said. She reached for a broom in case the lizard got loose, but the broom was too fast for Nina. It danced out of her grasp and boogied around the closet. A mop and bucket joined the broom, zigzagging between Nina, Cassidy, and Jeff.

"What's happening?" Nina squealed.

"We want to play orange ball," a voice chanted.

"It's Ozzy," Cassidy said. She ducked as a bucket sailed over her head.

"WE WANT TO PLAY! WE WANT TO PLAY!" Voices chanted from all around the kids.

"He's not alone!" Nina yelled. She dodged a dancing mop and desperately tried to pull open the door.

"I can't play!" Jeff yelled at the bouncing broom. "Because of you, my ball was taken away!"

An unseen hand tossed a bucket of water in Jeff's face. "Bleck!" Jeff screamed and wiped at the water with his free hand. "I wouldn't play with you if you were the last ghost on earth!"

But the mops didn't stop dancing. The buckets didn't stop flying and the brooms didn't stop bouncing. "WE WANT TO PLAY! WE WANT TO PLAY!" was chanted over and over.

Nina put her hands over her ears to drown out the noise, but she couldn't take it anymore. "All right!" she screamed. "You can play!"

The brooms, mops, and buckets fell to the ground and, for a moment, there was silence. Then one tiny voice asked, "When?"

Nina took a deep breath and said, "Soon."

Slowly, the door to the storage closet swung open and before anyone could say boo, the kids and the iguana raced back to their classroom . . .

About the Authors

Marcia Thornton Jones and Debbie Dadey got into the *spirit* of writing when they worked together at the same school in Lexington, Kentucky. Since then, Debbie has *haunted* several states. She currently *haunts* Ft. Collins, CO, with her three children, two dogs, and husband. Marcia remains in Lexington, KY where she lives with her husband and two cats. Debbie and Marcia have fun with spooky stories. They have scared themselves silly with *The Adventures of the Bailey School Kids* and *The Bailey City Monsters* series.